UP TO TEN AND DOWN AGAIN

LISA
CAMPBELL
ERNST

LOTHROP,
LEE & SHEPARD
BOOKS
·
NEW YORK

For Kevin
and Marshall

Printed in Hong Kong
First Edition 3 4 5 6 7 8 9 10
Library of Congress Cataloging in Publication
Data
Ernst, Lisa Campbell.
  Up to ten and down again.
    1. Children's stories, American. [1. Picnicking
—Fiction. 2. Stories without words. 3. Counting]
I. Title. PZ7.E7323Up 1986   [E]   84-21852
ISBN 0-688-04541-3   ISBN 0-688-04542-1 (lib. bdg.)

1

duck

2
cars

3
dogs

4
boys

5
girls

6

balls

7
boats

8 baskets

9
hats

10 clouds

10
clouds

9 hats

8
baskets

7
boats

6
balls

5
girls

4
boys

3 dogs

2 cars

1

duck

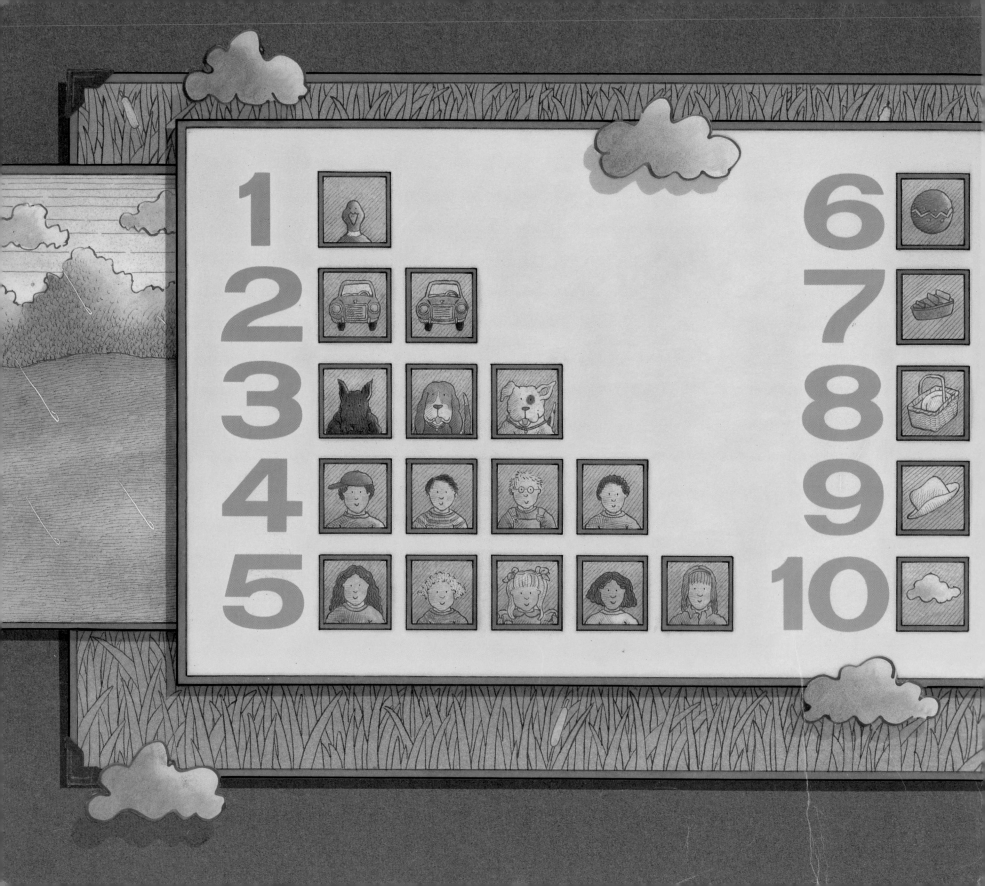